The Automaton

By

E. T. A. Hoffmann

British Library Cataloguing-in-Publication Data
A catalogue record for this book is available from the
British Library

E. T. A. Hoffman

Ernst Theodor Wilhelm Hoffmann was born in Königsberg, East Prussia in 1776. His family were all jurists, and during his youth he was initially encouraged to pursue a career in law. However, in his late teens Hoffman became increasingly interested in literature and philosophy, and spent much of his time reading German classicists and attending lectures by, amongst others, Immanuel Kant.

In was in his twenties, upon moving with his uncle to Berlin, that Hoffman first began to promote himself as a composer, writing an operetta called Die Maske and entering a number of playwriting competitions. Hoffman struggled to establish himself anywhere for a while, flitting between a number of cities and dodging the attentions of Napoleon's occupying troops. In 1808, while living in Bamberg, he began his job as a theatre manager and a music critic, and Hoffman's break came a year later, with the publication of Ritter Gluck. The story centred on a man who meets, or thinks he has met, a long-dead composer, and played into the 'doppelgänger' theme – at that time very popular in literature. It was shortly after this that Hoffman began to use the pseudonym E. T. A. Hoffmann, declaring the 'A' to stand for 'Amadeus', as a tribute to the great composer, Mozart.

Over the next decade, while moving between Dresden, Leipzig and Berlin, Hoffman produced a great range of both literary and musical works. Probably Hoffman's most well-known story, produced in 1816, is 'The Nutcracker and the Mouse King', due to the fact that – some seventy-six years later - it inspired Tchaikovsky's ballet The Nutcracker.

In the same vein, his story 'The Sandman' provided both the inspiration for Léo Delibes's ballet Coppélia, and the basis for a highly influential essay by Sigmund Freud, called 'The Uncanny'. (Indeed, Freud referred to Hoffman as the "unrivalled master of the uncanny in literature.")

Alcohol abuse and syphilis eventually took a great toll on Hoffman though, and – having spent the last year of his life paralysed – he died in Berlin in 1822, aged just 46. His legacy is a powerful one, however: He is seen as a pioneer of both Romanticism and fantasy literature, and his novella, Mademoiselle de Scudéri: A Tale from the Times of Louis XIV is often cited as the first ever detective story.

The Automaton

""The talking Turk" was attracting universal attention, and setting the town in commotion. The hall where this automaton was exhibited was thronged by a continual stream of visitors, of all sorts and conditions, from morning till night, all eager to listen to the oracular utterances which were whispered to them by the motionless lips of that wonderful quasi-human figure. The manner of the construction and arrangement of this automaton distinguished it in a marked degree from all puppets of the sort usually exhibited. It was, in fact, a very remarkable automaton. About the centre of a room of moderate size, containing only a few indispensable articles of furniture, at this figure, about the size of a human being, handsomely formed, dressed in a rich and tasteful Turkish costume, on a low seat shaped as a tripod, which the exhibitor would move if desired, to show that there was no means of communication between it and the ground. Its left hand was placed in an easy position on its knee, and its right rested on a small movable table. Its appearance, as has been said, was that of a well-proportioned, handsome man, but the most remarkable part of it was its head. A face expressing a genuine Oriental astuteness gave it an appearance of life rarely seen in wax figures, even when they represent the characteristic countenances of talented men. A light railing surrounded the figure, to prevent the spectators from crowding too closely about it; and only those who wished to inspect the construction of it (so far as the Exhibitor could allow this to be seen without divulging his secret), and the person whose turn it was to put a question to it, were allowed to go inside this railing, and close up to it. The usual mode of procedure was to whisper the question you wished to ask into the Turk's right ear; on which he would turn, first his eyes, and then his whole head, towards you; and as you were sensible of a gentle stream of air, like breath coming from his lips, you could not but suppose that the low reply which was given to you did really proceed from the interior of the figure. From time to time, after a few answers had been given, the Exhibitor would apply a key to the Turk's left side, and wind up some clockwork with a good deal of noise. Here, also, he would, if desired, open a species of lid, so that you could see inside the figure a complicated piece of mechanism consisting of a number of wheels; and although you might not think it probable that this had anything to do with the speaking of the automaton, still it was evident that it occupied so much space that no human being could possibly be concealed inside, were he no bigger than Augustus's dwarf who was served up in a pasty. Besides the movement of the head, which always took place before an answer was given, the Turk would sometimes also raise his right hand, and either make a warning gesture with the finger, or, as it were, motion the question away with the whole hand. When this happened, nothing but repeated urging by the questioner could extract an answer, which was then generally ambiguous or angry. It might have been that the wheel work was connected with, or answerable for, those motions of the head and hands, although even in this the agency of a sentient being seemed essential. People wearied themselves with conjectures concerning the source and agent of this marvellous Intelligence. The walls, the adjoining room, the furniture, everything connected with the exhibition, were carefully examined and scrutinised, all completely in vain. The figure and its Exhibitor were watched and scanned most closely by the eyes of the most expert in mechanical science; but the more close and minute the scrutiny, the more easy and unconstrained were the actions and proceedings of both. The Exhibitor laughed and joked in the furthest corner of the room with the spectators, leaving the figure to make its gestures and give its replies as a wholly independent thing, having no need of any connection with him. Indeed he could not wholly restrain a slightly ironical smile when the table and the figure and tripod were being overhauled and peered at in every direction, taken as close to the light as possible, and inspected by powerful magnifying glasses. The upshot of it all was, that the mechanical geniuses said the devil himself could make neither head nor tail of the confounded mechanism. And a hypothesis that the Exhibitor was a clever ventriloquist, and gave the answers himself (the breath being conveyed to the figure's mouth through hidden valves) fell to the ground, for the Exhibitor was to be heard talking loudly and distinctly to people among the audience at the very time when the Turk was making his replies.

"'Notwithstanding the enigmatical, and apparently mysterious, character of this exhibition, perhaps the interest of the public might soon have grown fainter, had it not been kept alive by the nature of the answers which the Turk gave. These were sometimes cold and severe, while occasionally they were sparkling and jocular--even broadly so at times; at others they evinced strong sense and deep astuteness, and in some instances they were in a high degree painful and tragical. But they were always strikingly apposite to the character and affairs of the questioner, who would frequently be startled by a mystical reference to futurity in the answer given, only possible, as it would seem, in one cognizant of the hidden thoughts and feelings which dictated the question. And it happened not seldom that the Turk, questioned in German, would reply in some other language known to the questioner, in which case it would be found that the answer could not have been expressed with equal point, force, and conciseness in any other language than that selected. In short, no day passed without some fresh instance of a striking and ingenious answer of the wise Turk becoming the subject of general remark.

"'It chanced, one evening, that Lewis and Ferdinand, two college friends, were in a company where the talking Turk was the subject of conversation. People were discussing whether the strangest feature of the matter was the mysterious and unexplained human influence which seemed to endow the figure with life, or the wonderful insight into the individuality of the questioner, or the remarkable talent of the answers. They were both rather ashamed to confess that they had not seen the Turk as yet, for it was de rigueur to see him, and every one had some tale to tell of a wonderful answer to some skilfully devised question.

""All figures of that description," said Lewis, "which can scarcely be said to counterfeit humanity so much as to travesty it--mere images of living death or inanimate life are in the highest degree hateful to me. When I was a little boy, I ran away crying from a waxwork exhibition I was taken to, and even to this day I never can enter a place of the sort without a horrible, eerie, shuddery feeling. When I see the staring, lifeless, glassy eyes of all the potentates, celebrated heroes, thieves, murderers, and so on, fixed upon me, I feel disposed to cry with Macbeth

"""Thou hast no speculation in those eyes

Which thou dost glare with.'

And I feel certain that most people experience the same feeling, though perhaps not to the same extent. For you may notice that scarcely any one talks, except in a whisper, in those waxwork places. You hardly ever hear a loud word. But it is not reverence for the Crowned Heads and other great people that produces this universal pianissimo; it is the oppressive sense of being in the presence of something unnatural and gruesome; and what I most of all detest is anything in the shape of imitation of the motions of Human Beings by machinery. I feel sure this wonderful, ingenious Turk will haunt me with his rolling eyes, his turning head, and his waving arm, like some necromantic goblin, when I lie awake of nights; so that the truth is I should very much prefer not going to see him. I should be quite satisfied with other people's accounts of his wit and wisdom."

""You know," said Ferdinand, "that I fully agree with you as to the disagreeable feeling produced by the sight of those imitations of Human Beings. But they are not all alike as regards that. Much depends on the workmanship of them, and on what they do. Now there was Ensler's rope dancer, one of the most perfect automatons I have ever seen. There was a vigour about his movements which was most effective, and when he suddenly sat down on his rope, and bowed in an affable manner, he was utterly delightful. I do not suppose any one ever experienced the gruesome feeling you speak of in looking at him. As for the Turk, I consider his case different altogether. The figure (which every one says is a handsome-looking one, with nothing ludicrous or repulsive about it) the figure really plays a very subordinate part in the business, and I think there can be little doubt that the turning of the head and eyes, and so forth, go on merely that our notice may be directed to them, for the very reason that it is elsewhere that the key to the mystery is to be found. That the breath comes out of the figure's mouth is very likely, perhaps certain; those who have been there say it does. It by no means follows that this breath is set in motion by the words which are spoken. There cannot be the smallest doubt that some human being is so placed as to be able, by means of acoustical and optical contrivances which we do not trace, to see and hear the persons who ask questions, and whisper answers back to them; that not a soul, even amongst our most ingenious mechanicians, has the slightest inkling, as yet, of the process by which this is done, shows that it is a remarkably ingenious one; and that, of course, is one thing which renders the exhibition very interesting. But much the most wonderful part of it, in my opinion, is the spiritual power of this unknown human being, who seems to read the very depths of the questioner's soul; the answers often display an acuteness and sagacity, and, at the same time, a species of dread half-light, half-darkness, which do really entitle them to be styled 'oracular' in the highest sense of the term. Several of my friends have told me instances of the sort which have fairly astounded me, and I can no longer refrain from putting the wonderful seer-gift of this unknown person to the test, so that I intend to go there to-morrow forenoon; and you must lay aside your repugnance to 'living puppets,' and come with me."

"'Although Lewis did his best to get off, he was obliged to yield, on pain of being considered eccentric, so many were the entreaties to him not to spoil a pleasant party by his absence, for a party had been made up to go the next forenoon, and, so to speak, take the miraculous Turk by the very beard. They went accordingly, and although there was no denying that the Turk had an unmistakable air of Oriental grandezza, and that his head was handsome and effective, yet, as soon as Lewis entered the room, he was struck with a sense of the ludicrous about the whole affair, and when the Exhibitor put the key to the figure's side, and the wheels began their whirring, he made some rather silly joke to his friends about "the Turkish gentleman's having a roasting-jack inside him."

Every one laughed; and the Exhibitor--who did not seem to appreciate the joke very much--stopped winding up the machinery. Whether it was that the hilarious mood of the company displeased the wise Turk, or that he chanced not to be "in the vein" on that particular day, his replies--though some were to very witty and ingenious questions--seemed empty and poor; and Lewis, in particular, had the misfortune to find that he was scarcely ever properly understood by the oracle, so that he received for the most part crooked answers. The Exhibitor was clearly out of temper, and the audience were on the point of going away, ill-pleased and disappointed, when Ferdinand said--

""Gentlemen, we none of us seem to be much satisfied with the wise Turk, but perhaps we may be partly to blame ourselves, probably our questions may not have been altogether to his taste; the fact that he is turning his head round at this moment, and raising his arm" (the figure was really doing so), "seems to indicate that I am not mistaken. A question has occurred to me to put to him; and if he gives one of his apposite answers to it, I think he will have quite redeemed his character."

"Ferdinand went up to the Turk, and whispered a word or two in his ear. The Turk raised his arm as unwilling to answer. Ferdinand persisted, and then the Turk turned his head towards him.

"Lewis saw that Ferdinand instantly turned pale; but after a few seconds he asked another question, to which he got an answer at once. It was with a most constrained smile

14

that Ferdinand, turning to the audience, said--

""'I can assure you, gentlemen, that as far as I am concerned at any rate, the Turk has redeemed his character. I must beg you to pardon me if I conceal the question and the answer from you; of course the secrets of the Oracle may not be divulged."

""Though Ferdinand strove hard to hide what he felt, it was but too evident from his efforts to be at ease that he was very deeply moved, and the cleverest answer could not have produced in the spectators the strange sensation, amounting to a species of awe, which his unmistakable emotion gave rise to in them. The fun and the jests were at an end; hardly another word was spoken, and the audience dispersed in uneasy silence.

""'Dear Lewis," said Ferdinand, as soon as they were alone together, "I must tell you all about this. The Turk has broken my heart; for I believe I shall never get over the blow he has given me until I do really die of the fulfilment of his terrible prophecy."

"'Lewis gazed at him in the profoundest amazement; and Ferdinand continued--

""'I see, now, that the mysterious being who communicates with us by the medium of the Turk, has powers at his command which compel our most secret thoughts with magic might; it may be that this strange intelligence clearly and distinctly beholds that germ of the future which fructifies within us in mysterious connection with the outer world, and is thus cognizant of all that is to come upon us in distant days, like those persons who are endowed with that unhappy seer-gift which enables them to predict the hour of death."

""You must have put an extraordinary question," Lewis answered; "but I should think you are tacking on some unduly important meaning to the Oracle's ambiguous reply. Mere chance, I should imagine, has educed something which is, by accident, appropriate to your question; and you are attributing this to the mystic power of the person (most probably quite an every-day sort of creature) who speaks to us through the Turk."

""What you say," answered Ferdinand, "is quite at variance with all the conclusions you and I have come to on the subject of what is ordinarily termed 'chance.' However, you cannot be expected to comprehend the precise condition in which I am, without my telling you all about an affair which happened to me some time ago, as to which I have never breathed a syllable to any one living till now. Several years ago I was on my way back to B----, from a place a long way off in East Prussia, belonging to my father. In K----, I met with some young Courland fellows who were going back to B---- too. We travelled together in three post carriages; and, as we had plenty of money, and were all about the time of life when people's spirits are pretty high, you may imagine the manner of our journey. We were continually playing the maddest pranks of every kind. I remember that we got to M---- about noon, and set to work to plunder the landlady's wardrobe. A crowd collected in front of the inn, and we marched up and down, dressed in some of her clothes, smoking, till the postilion's horn sounded, and off we set again. We reached D---- in the highest possible spirits, and were so delighted with the place and scenery, that we determined to stay there several days. We made a number of excursions in the neighbourhood, and so once, when we had been out all day at the Karlsberg, finding a grand bowl of punch waiting for us on our return, we dipped into it pretty freely. Although I had not taken more of it than was good for me, still, I had been in the grand sea-breeze all day, and I felt all my pulses throbbing, and my blood seemed to rush through my veins in a stream of fire. When we went to our rooms at last, I threw myself down on my bed; but, tired as I was, my sleep was scarcely more than a kind of dreamy, half-conscious condition, in which I was cognizant of all that was going on about me. I fancied I could hear soft conversation in the next room, and at last I plainly made out a male voice saying--

"""Well, good night, now; mind and be ready in good time.'

"""A door opened and closed again, and then came a deep silence; but this was soon broken by one or two chords of a pianoforte.

"""You know the magical effect of music sounding in that way in the stillness of night. I felt as though some beautiful spirit voice was speaking to me in these chords. I lay listening, expecting something in the shape of a fantasia--or some such piece of music--to follow; but fancy what it was when a most gloriously, exquisitely beautiful lady's voice sang, to a

17

melody that went to one's very heart, the words I am going to repeat to you--

    ""'Mio ben ricordati
    S' avvien ch' io mora
    Quanto quest' anima
    Fedel t' amo;
    Lo se pur amano
    Le fredde ceneri,
    Nel urna ancora
    T' adorero'."3

    ""'How can I ever hope to give you the faintest idea of the effect of those long-drawn swelling and dying notes upon me. I had never imagined anything approaching it. The melody was marvellous--quite unlike any other. It was, itself, the deep, tender sorrow of the most fervent love. As it rose in simple phrases, the clear upper notes like crystal bells, and sank till the rich low tunes died away like the sighs of a despairing plaint, a rapture which words cannot describe took possession of me--the pain of a boundless longing seized my heart like a spasm; I could scarcely breathe, my whole being was merged in an inexpressible, super-earthly delight. I did not dare to move; could only listen; soul and body were merged in ear. It was not until the tones had been for some time silent that tears, coming to my eyes, broke the spell, and restored me to myself. I suppose that sleep then came upon me, for when I was roused by the shrill notes of a posthorn, the bright morning sun was shining into my room, and I found that it had been only in my dreams that I had been enjoying a bliss more deep, a happiness more ineffable, than the world could otherwise have afforded me. For a beautiful lady came to me--it was the lady who had sung the song--and said to me, very fondly and tenderly--

"""Then you did recognize me, my own dear Ferdinand! I knew that I had only to sing, and I should live again in you wholly, for every note was sleeping in your heart.'

"""Then I recognized, with rapture unspeakable, that she was the beloved of my soul, whose image had been enshrined in my heart since childhood. Though an adverse fate had torn her from me for a time, I had found her again now; but my deep and fervent love for her melted into that wonderful melody of sorrow, and our words and our looks grew into exquisite swelling tones of music, flowing together into a river of fire. Now, however, that I had awakened from this beautiful dream, I was obliged to confess to myself that I could trace no association of former days connected with it. I never had seen the beautiful lady before.

"""I heard some one talking loudly and angrily in front of the house, and rising mechanically, I went to the window. An elderly gentleman, well dressed, was rating the postilion, who had damaged something about an elegant travelling carriage; at last this was put to rights, and the gentleman called upstairs to some one, 'We're all ready now; come along, it's time to be off.' I found that there had been a young lady looking out of the window next to mine; but as she drew quickly back, and had on a broad travelling hat, I did not see her face; when she went out, she turned round and looked up at me. Heavens! she was the singer! she was the lady of my dream! For a moment her beautiful eyes rested upon me, and the beam of a crystal tone seemed to pierce my heart like the point of a burning dagger, so that I felt an actual physical smart: all my members trembled, and I was transfixed with an indescribable bliss. She got quickly into the carriage, the postilion blew a cheerful tune as if in jubilant defiance, and in a moment they had disappeared round the corner of the street. I remained at the window like a man in a dream. My Courland friends came in to fetch me for an excursion which had been arranged: I never spoke; they thought I was ill. How could I have uttered a single word connected with what had occurred? I abstained from making any inquiries in the hotel about the occupants of the room next to mine; I felt that every word relating to her uttered by any lips but mine would be a desecration of my tender secret. I resolved to keep it always faithfully from thenceforth, to bear it about with me always, and to be for ever true to her--my only love for evermore--although I might never see her again. You can quite understand my feelings. I know you will not blame me for having immediately given up everybody and everything but the most eager search for the very slightest trace of my unknown love. My jovial Courland friends were now perfectly unendurable to me; I slipped away from them quietly in the night, and was off as fast as I could travel to B----, to go on with my work there. You know I was always pretty good at drawing. Well, in B---- I took lessons in miniature painting from good masters, and got on so well that in a short time I was able to carry out the idea which had set me on this tack--to paint a portrait of her, as like as it could be made. I worked at it secretly, with locked doors. No human eye has ever seen it; for I had another picture the exact size of it framed, and put her portrait into the frame instead of it, myself. Ever since, I have worn it next my heart.

""I have never mentioned this affair--much the most important event in my life--until to-day; and you are the only creature in the world, Lewis, to whom I have breathed a word of my secret. Yet this very day a hostile influence--I know not whence or what--comes piercing into my heart and life! When I went up to the Turk, I asked--thinking of my beloved--

"""Will there ever be a time again for me like that which was the happiest in my life?'

"""The Turk was most unwilling to answer me, as I daresay you observed; but at last, as I persisted, he said--

"""I am looking into your breast; but the glitter of the gold, which is towards me, distracts me. Turn the picture round.'

"""Have I words for the feeling which went shuddering through me? I am sure you must have seen how I was startled. The picture was really placed on my breast in the way the Turk had said; I turned it round, unobserved, and repeated my question. Then the figure said, in a sorrowful tone--

"""Unhappy man! At the very moment when next you

see her, she will be lost to you for ever!'"

"'Lewis was about to try to cheer his friend, who had fallen into a deep reverie, but some mutual acquaintances came in, and they were interrupted.

"'The story of this fresh instance of a mysterious answer by the Turk spread in the town, and people busied themselves in conjectures as to the unfavourable prophecy which had so upset the unprejudiced Ferdinand. His friends were besieged with questions, and Lewis had to invent a marvellous tale, which had all the more universal a success that it was remote from the truth. The coterie of people with whom Ferdinand had been induced to go and see the Turk was in the habit of meeting once a week, and at their next meeting the Turk was necessarily the topic of conversation, as efforts were continually being made to obtain, from Ferdinand himself, full particulars of an adventure which had thrown him into such an evident despondency. Lewis felt most deeply how bitter a blow it was to Ferdinand to find the secret of his romantic love, preserved so long and faithfully, penetrated by a fearful, unknown power; and he, like Ferdinand, was almost convinced that the mysterious link which attaches the present to the future must be clear to the vision of that power to which the most hidden secrets were thus manifest. Lewis could not help believing the Oracle; but the malevolence, the relentlessness with which the misfortune impending over his friend had been announced, made him indignant with the undiscovered Being which spoke by the mouth of the Turk, so that he placed himself in persistent opposition to the Automaton's many admirers; and whilst they considered that there was much impressiveness about its most natural movements, enhancing the effect of its oracular sayings, he maintained that it was those very turnings of the head and rollings of the eyes which he considered so absurd, and that this was the reason why he could not help making a joke on the subject; a joke which had put the Exhibitor out of temper, and probably the invisible agent as well. Indeed the latter had shown that this was so by giving a number of stupid and unmeaning answers.

""I must tell you," said Lewis, "that the moment I went into the room the figure reminded me of a most delightful Nutcracker which a cousin of mine once gave me at Christmas time when I was a little boy. The little fellow had the gravest and most comical face ever seen, and when he had a hard nut to crack there was some arrangement inside him which made him roll his great eyes, which projected far out of his head, and this gave him such an absurdly life-like effect that I could play with him for hours; in fact, in my secret soul, I almost thought he was real. All the marionettes I have seen since then, however perfect, I have thought stiff and lifeless compared to my glorious Nutcracker. I had heard much of some wonderful automatons in the Arsenal at Dantzig, and I took care to go and see them when I was there some years ago. Soon after I got into the place where they were, an old-fashioned German soldier came marching up to me, and fired off his musket with such a bang that the great vaulted hall rang again. There were other similar tricks which I forget about now; but at length I was taken into a room where I found the God of War--the terrible Mars himself--with all his suite. He was seated, in a rather grotesque dress, on a throne ornamented with arms of all sorts; heralds and warriors were standing round him. As soon as we came before the throne, a set of drummers began to roll their drums, and lifers blew on their fifes in the most horrible way--all out of tune--so that one had to put one's fingers in one's ears. My remark was that the God of War was very badly off for a band, and every one agreed with me. The drums and fifes stopped; the heralds began to turn their heads about, and stamp with their halberds, and finally the God of War, after rolling his eyes for a time, started up from his seat, and seemed to be coming straight at us. However, he soon sank back on his throne again, and after a little more drumming and fifing, everything reverted to its state of wooden repose. As I came away from seeing these automatons, I said to myself, 'Nothing like my Nutcracker!' And now that I have seen the sage Turk, I say again, 'Give me my Nutcracker.'

""People laughed at this, of course; though it was believed to be 'more jest than earnest,' for, to say nothing of the remarkable cleverness of many of the Turk's answers, the indiscoverable connection between him and the hidden Being who, besides speaking through him, must produce the movements which accompanied his answers, was unquestionably very wonderful, at all events a masterpiece of mechanical and acoustical skill."

"'Lewis was himself obliged to admit this; and every one was extolling the inventor of the automaton, when an elderly gentleman who, as a general rule, spoke very little, and had been taking no part in the conversation on the present occasion, rose from his chair (as he was in the habit of doing when he did finally say a few words, always greatly to the point) and began, in his usual polite manner, as follows--

"'"Will you be good enough to allow me, gentlemen--I beg you to pardon me. You have reason to admire the curious work of art which has been interesting us all for so long; but you are wrong in supposing the commonplace person who exhibits it to be the inventor of it. The truth is that he really has no hand at all in what are the truly remarkable features of it. The originator of them is a gentleman highly skilled in matters of the kind--one who lives amongst us, and has done so for many years--whom we all know very well, and greatly respect and esteem."

"Universal surprise was created by this, and the elderly gentleman was besieged with questions, on which he continued;

"'"The gentleman to whom I allude is none other than Professor X----. The Turk had been here a couple of days, and nobody had taken any particular notice of him, though Professor X--- took care to go and see him at once, because everything in the shape of an Automaton interests him in the highest degree. When he had heard one or two of the Turk's answers, he took the Exhibitor apart and whispered a word or two in his ear. The man turned pale, and shut up his exhibition as soon as the two or three people who were then in the room had gone away. The bills disappeared from the walls, and nothing more was heard of the Talking Turk for a fortnight. Then new bills came out, and the Turk was found with the fine new head, and all the other arrangements as they are at present--an unsolvable riddle. It is since that time that his answers have been so clever and so interesting. But that all this is the work of Professor X---- admits of no question. The Exhibitor, in the interval, when the figure was not being exhibited, spent all his time with him. Also it is well known that the Professor passed several days in succession in the room where the figure is. Besides, gentlemen, you are no doubt aware that the Professor himself possesses a number of most extraordinary automatons, chiefly musical, which he has long vied with Hofrath B---- in producing, keeping up with him a correspondence concerning all sorts of mechanical, and, people say, even magical arts and pursuits, and that, did he but choose, he could astonish the world with them. But he works in complete privacy, although he is always ready to show his extraordinary inventions to all who take a real interest in such matters."

"It was, in fact, matter of notoriety that this Professor X----, whose principal pursuits were natural philosophy and chemistry, delighted, next to them, in occupying himself with mechanical research; but no one in the assemblage had had the slightest idea that he had had any connection with the "Talking Turk," and it was from the merest hearsay that people knew anything concerning the curiosities which the old gentleman had referred to. Ferdinand and Lewis felt strangely and vividly impressed by the old gentleman's account of Professor X----, and the influence which he had brought to bear on that strange automaton.

""I cannot hide from you," said Ferdinand, "that a hope is dawning upon me that, if I get nearer to this Professor X----, I may, perhaps, come upon a clue to the mystery which is weighing so terribly upon me at present. And it is possible that the true significance and import of the relations which exist between the Turk (or rather the hidden entity which employs him as the organ of its oracular utterances) and myself might, could I get to comprehend it, perhaps comfort me, and weaken the impression of those words, for me so terrible. I have made up my mind to make the acquaintance of this mysterious man, on the pretext of seeing his automatons; and as they are musical ones, it will not be devoid of interest for you to come with me."

""As if it were not sufficient for me," said Lewis, "to be able to aid you, in your necessity, with counsel and help! But I cannot deny that even to-day, when the old gentleman was mentioning Professor X----'s connection with the Turk, strange ideas came into my mind; although perhaps I am going a long way about in search of what lies close at hand, could one but see it. For instance, to look as close at hand as possible for the solution of the mystery, may it not be the case that the invisible being knew that you wore the picture next your heart, so that a mere lucky guess might account for the rest? Perhaps it was taking its revenge upon you for the

27

rather uncourteous style in which we were joking about the Turk's wisdom."

""'Not one human soul," Ferdinand answered, "has ever set eyes on the picture; this I told you before. And I have never told any creature but yourself of the adventure which has had such an immensely important influence on my whole life. It is an utter impossibility that the Turk can have got to know of this in any ordinary manner. Much more probably, what you say you are 'going a long roundabout way' in search of may be much nearer the truth."

""'Well then," said Lewis, "what I mean is this; that this automaton, strongly as I appeared to-day to assert the contrary, is really one of the most extraordinary phenomena ever beheld, and that everything goes to prove that whoever controls and directs it has at his command higher powers than is supposed by those who go there simply to gape at things, and do no more than wonder at what is wonderful. The figure is nothing more than the outward form of the communication; but that form has been cleverly selected, as such, since the shape, appearance, and movements of it are well adapted to occupy the attention in a manner favourable for the preservation of the secret, and, particularly, to work upon the questioners favourably as regards the intelligence, whatsoever it is, which gives the answers. There cannot be any human being concealed inside the figure; that is as good as proved, so that it is clearly the result of some acoustic deception that we think the answers come from the Turk's mouth. But how this is accomplished--how the Being who gives the answers is placed in a position to hear the questions and see the questioners, and at the same time to be audible by them--certainly remains a complete mystery to me. Of course all this merely implies great acoustic and mechanical skill on the part of the inventor, and remarkable acuteness, or, I might say, systematic craftiness, in leaving no stone unturned in the process of deceiving us. And I admit that this part of the riddle interests me the less, inasmuch as it falls completely into the shade in comparison with the circumstance (which, is the only part of the affair which is so extraordinarily remarkable) that the Turk often reads the very soul of the questioner. How, if it were possible to this Being which gives the answers, to acquire by some process unknown to us, a psychic influence over us, and to place itself in a spiritual rapport with us, so that it can comprehend and read our minds and thoughts, and more than that, have cognizance of our whole inner being; so that, if it does not clearly speak out the secrets which are lying dormant within us, it does yet evoke and call forth, in a species of extasis induced by its rapport with the exterior spiritual principle, the suggestions, the outlines, the shadowings of all which is reposing within our breasts, clearly seen by the eye of the spirit, in brightest illumination! On this assumption the psychical power would strike the strings within us, so as to make them give forth a clear and vibrating chord, audible to us, and intelligible by us, instead of merely murmuring, as they do at other times; so that it is we who answer our own selves; the voice which we hear is produced from within ourselves by the operation of this unknown spiritual power, and vague presentiments and anticipations of the future brighten into spoken prognostications--just as, in dreams, we often find that a voice, unfamiliar to us, tells us of things which we do not know, or as to which we are in doubt, being, in reality, a voice proceeding from ourselves, although it seems to convey to us knowledge which previously we did not possess. No doubt the Turk (that is to say, the hidden power which is connected with him) seldom finds it necessary to place himself en rapport with people in this way. Hundreds of them can be dealt with in the cursory, superficial manner adapted to their queries and characters, and it is seldom that a question is put which calls for the exercise of anything besides ready wit. But by any strained or exalted condition of the questioner the Turk would be affected in quite a different way, and he would then employ those means which render possible the production of a psychic rapport, giving him the power to answer from out of the inner depths of the questioner. His hesitation in replying to deep questions of this kind may be due to the delay which he grants himself to gain a few moments for the bringing into play of the power in question. This is my true and genuine opinion; and you see that I have not that contemptuous notion of this work of art (or whatever may be the proper term to apply to it) that I would have had you believe I had. But I do not wish to conceal anything from you; though I see that if you adopt my idea, I shall not have given you any real comfort at all."

""You are wrong there, dear friend," said Ferdinand.

"The very fact that your opinion does chime in with a vague notion which I felt, dimly, in my own mind, comforts me very much. It is only myself that I have to take into account; my precious secret is not discovered, for 1 know that you will guard it as a sacred treasure. And, by-the-bye, I must tell you of a most extraordinary feature of the matter, which I had forgotten till now. Just as the Turk was speaking his latter words, I fancied that I heard one or two broken phrases of the sorrowful melody, 'mio ben ricordati,' and then it seemed to me that one single, long-drawn note of the glorious voice which I heard on that eventful night went floating by."

""Well," said Lewis, "and I remember, too, that, just as your answer was being given to you, I happened to place my hand on the railing which surrounds the figure. I felt it thrill and vibrate in my hand, and I fancied also that I could hear a kind of musical sound, for I cannot say it was a vocal note, passing across the room. I paid no attention to it, because, as you know, my head is always full of music, and I have several times been wonderfully deceived in a similar way; but I was very much astonished, in my own mind, when I traced the mysterious connection between that sound and your adventure in D----."

"'The fact that Lewis had heard the sound as well as himself, was to Ferdinand a proof of the psychic rapport which existed between them; and as they further diseased the marvels of the affair, he began to feel the heavy burden which had weighed upon him since he heard the fatal answer lifted away, and was ready to go forward bravely to meet whatsoever the future might have in store.

""It is impossible that I can lose her," he said. "She is my heart's queen, and will always be there, as long as my own life endures."

"'They went and called on Professor X----, in high hope that he would be able to throw light on many questions relating to occult sympathies and the like, in which they were deeply interested. They found him to be an old man, dressed in old-fashioned French style, exceedingly keen and lively, with small grey eyes which had an unpleasant way of fixing themselves on one, and a sarcastic simile, not very attractive, playing about his mouth.

"'When they had expressed their wish to see some of his automatons, he said, "Ah! and you really take an interest in mechanical matters, do you? Perhaps you have done something in that direction yourselves? Well, I can show you, in this house here, what you will look for in vain in the rest of Europe: I may say, in the known world."

"'There was something most unpleasant about the Professor's voice; it was a high-pitched, screaming sort of discordant tenor, exactly suited to the mountebank tone in which he proclaimed his treasures. He fetched his keys with a great clatter, and opened the door of a tastefully and elegantly furnished hall, where the automatons were. There was a piano in the middle of the loom, on a raised platform; beside it, on the right, a life-sized figure of a man, with a flute in his hand; on the left, a female figure, seated at an instrument somewhat resembling a piano; behind her were two boys, with a drum and a triangle. In the background our two friends noticed an orchestrion (which was an instrument already known to them), and all round the walls were a number of musical clocks. The Professor passed, in a cursory manner, close by the orchestrion and the clocks, and just touched the automatons, almost imperceptibly; then he sat down at the piano, and began to play, pianissimo, an andante in the style of a march. He played it once through by himself; and as he commenced it for the second time the flute-player put his instrument to his lips, and took up the melody; then one of the boys drummed softly on his drum in the most accurate time, and the other just touched his triangle, so that you could hear it and no more. Presently the lady came in with full chords, of a sound something like those of a harmonica, which she produced by pressing down the keys of her instrument; and now the whole room kept growing more and more alive; the musical clocks came in one by one, with the utmost rhythmical precision; the boy drummed louder; the triangle rang through the room, and lastly the orchestrion set to work, and drummed and trumpeted fortissimo, so that the whole place shook again; and this went on till the Professor wound up the whole business with one final chord, all the machines finishing also, with the utmost precision. Our friends bestowed the applause which the Professor's complacent smile (with its undercurrent of sarcasm) seemed to demand of them. He went up to the figures to set about exhibiting some further similar musical feats; but Lewis and Ferdinand, as if by a preconcerted arrangement, declared that they had pressing business which prevented their making a longer stay, and took their leave of the inventor and his machines.

""'Most interesting and ingenious, wasn't it?" said Ferdinand; but Lewis's anger, long restrained, broke out.

""'Oh! confusion on that wretched Professor!" he cried. "What a terrible, terrible disappointment! Where are all the revelations we expected? What became of the learned, instructive discourse which we thought he would deliver to us, as to disciples at Sais?"

""'At the same time," said Ferdinand, "we have seen some very ingenious mechanical inventions, curious and interesting from a musical point of view. Clearly, the flute-player is the same as Vaucanson's well-known machine; and a similar mechanism applied to the fingers of the female figure is, I suppose, what enables her to bring out those really beautiful tones from her instrument. The way in which all the machines work together is really astonishing."

""'It is exactly that which drives me so wild," said Lewis. "All that machine-music (in which I include the Professor's own playing) makes every bone in my body ache. I am sure I do not know when I shall get over it! The fact of any human being's doing anything in association with those lifeless figures which counterfeit the appearance and movements of humanity has always, to me, something fearful, unnatural, T may say terrible, about it. I suppose it would be possible, by means of certain mechanical arrangements inside them, to construct automatons which should dance, and then to set them to dance with human beings, and twist and turn about in all sorts of figures; so that we should have a living man putting his arms about a lifeless partner of wood, and whirling round and round with her, or rather it. Could you look at such a sight, for an instant, without horror? At all events, all machine-music is to me a thing altogether monstrous and abominable; and a good stocking-loom is, in my opinion, worth all the most perfect and ingenious musical clocks in the universe put together. For is it the breath, merely, of the performer on a wind-instrument, or the skilful, supple fingers of the performer on a stringed instrument, which evoke those tones which lay upon us a spell of such power, and awaken that inexpressible feeling, akin to nothing else on earth, the sense of a distant spirit world, and of our own higher life therein? Is it not, rather, the mind, the soul, the heart, which merely employ those bodily organs to give forth into our external life that which is felt in our inner depths? so that it can be communicated to others, and awaken kindred chords in them, opening, in harmonious echoes, that marvellous kingdom from whence those tones come darting, like beams of light? To set to work to make music by means of valves, springs, levers, cylinders, or whatever other apparatus you choose to employ, is a senseless attempt to make the means to an end accomplish what can result only when those means are animated and, in their minutest movements, controlled by the mind, the soul, and the heart. The gravest reproach you can make to a musician is that he plays without expression; because, by so doing, he is marring the whole essence of the matter. Yet the coldest and most unfeeling executant will always be far in advance of the most perfect of machines. For it is impossible that no impulse whatever, from the inner man shall ever, even for a moment, animate his rendering; whereas, in the case of a machine, no such impulse can ever do so. The attempts of mechanicians to imitate, with more or less approximation to accuracy, the human organs in the production of musical sounds, or to substitute mechanical appliances for those organs, I consider tantamount to a declaration of war against the spiritual element in music; but the greater the forces they array against it, the more victorious it is. For this very reason, the more perfect that this sort of machinery is, the more I disapprove of it; and I infinitely prefer the commonest barrel-organ, in which the mechanism attempts nothing but to be mechanical, to Vaucauson's flute-player, or the harmonica girl.

"""I entirely agree with you," said Ferdinand, "and indeed you have merely put into words what I have always thought; and I was much struck with it to-day at the Professor's. Although I do not so wholly live and move and have my being in music as you do, and consequently am not so sensitively alive to imperfections in it, I, too, have always felt a repugnance to the stiffness and lifelessness of machine-music; and, I can remember, when I was a child at home, how I detested a large, ordinary musical clock, which played its little tune every hour. It is a pity that those skilful mechanicians do not try to apply their knowledge to the improvement of musical instruments, rather than to puerilities of this sort."

""Exactly," said Lewis. "Now, in the case of instruments of the keyboard class a great deal might be done. There is a wide field open in that direction to clever mechanical people, much as has been accomplished already; particularly in instruments of the pianoforte genus. But it would be the task of a really advanced system of the 'mechanics of music' to closely observe, minutely study, and carefully discover that class of sounds which belong, most purely and strictly, to Nature herself, to obtain a knowledge of the tones which dwell in substances of every description, and then to take this mysterious music and enclose it in some description of instrument, where it should be subject to man's will, and give itself forth at his touch. All the attempts to bring music out of metal or glass cylinders, glass threads, slips of glass, or pieces of marble; or to cause strings to vibrate or sound, in ways unlike the ordinary ways, seem to me to be interesting in the highest degree: and what stands in the way of our real progress in the discovery of the marvellous acoustical secrets which lie hidden all around us in nature is, that every imperfect attempt at an experiment is at once held up to laudation as being a new and utterly perfect invention, either for vanity's sake, or for money's. This is why so many new instruments have started into existence--most of them with grand or ridiculous names--and have disappeared and been forgotten just as quickly."

""Your 'higher mechanics of music' seems to be a most interesting subject," said Ferdinand, "although, for my part, I do not as yet quite perceive the object at which it aims."

""The object at which it aims," said Lewis, "is the discovery of the most absolutely perfect kind of musical sound; and according to my theory, musical sound would be the nearer to perfection the more closely it approximated to such of the mysterious tones of nature as are not wholly dissociated from this earth."

""I presume," said Ferdinand, "that it is because I have not penetrated so deeply into this subject as you have, but you must allow me to say that I do not quite understand you."

""Then," said Lewis, "let me give you some sort of an idea how it is that all this question exhibits itself to my mind.

""In the primeval condition of the human race, while (to make use of almost the very words of a talented writer--Schubert--in his 'Glimpses at the Night Side of Natural Science') mankind as yet was dwelling in its pristine holy harmony with nature, richly endowed with a heavenly instinct of prophecy and poetry; while, as yet, Mother Nature continued to nourish from the fount of her own life, the wondrous being to whom she had given birth, she encompassed him with a holy music, like the afflatus of a continual inspiration; and wondrous tones spake of the mysteries of her unceasing activity. There has come down to us an echo from the mysterious depths of those primeval days--that beautiful notion of the music of the spheres, which, when as a boy, I first read of it in 'The Dream of Scipio,' filled me with the deepest and most devout reverence. I often used to listen, on quiet moonlight nights, to hear if those wondrous tones would come to me, borne on the wings of the whispering airs. However, as I said to you already, those nature-tones have not yet all departed from this world, fur we have an instance of their survival, and occurrence in that 'Music of the Air' or 'Voice of the Demon,' mentioned by a writer on Ceylon--a sound which so powerfully affects the human system, that even the least impressionable persons, when they hear those tones of nature imitating, in such a terrible manner, the expression of human sorrow and suffering, are struck with painful compassion and profound terror! Indeed, I once met with an instance of a phenomenon of a similar kind myself, at a place in East Prussia. I had been living there for some time; it was about the end of autumn, when, on quiet nights, with a moderate breeze blowing, I used distinctly to hear tones, sometimes resembling the deep, stopped, pedal pipe of an organ, and sometimes like the vibrations from a deep, soft-toned bell. I often distinguished, quite clearly, the low F, and the fifth above it (the C), and not seldom the minor third above, E flat, was perceptible as well; and then this tremendous chord of the seventh, so woeful and so solemn, produced on one the effect of the most intense sorrow, and even of terror!

""There is, about the imperceptible commencement, the swelling and the gradual dying of those nature-tones a something which has a most powerful and indescribable effect upon us; and any instrument which should be capable of producing this would, no doubt, affect us in a similar way. So that I think the harmonica comes the nearest, as regards its tone, to that perfection, which is to be measured by its influence on our minds. And it is fortunate that this instrument (which chances to be the very one which imitates those nature-tones with such exactitude) happens to be just the very one which is incapable of lending itself to frivolity or ostentation, but exhibits its characteristic qualities in the purest of simplicity. The recently invented 'harmonichord' will doubtless accomplish much in this direction. This instrument, as you no doubt know, sets strings a-vibrating and a-toning (not bells, as in the harmonica) by means of mechanism, which is set in motion by the pressing down of keys, and the rotation of a cylinder. The performer has, under his control, the commencement, the swelling out, and the diminishing, of the tones much more than is the case with the harmonica, though as yet the harmonichord has not the tone of the harmonica, which sounds as if it came straight from another world."

""I have heard that instrument," said Ferdinand, "and certainly the tone of it went to the very depths of my being, although I thought the performer was doing it scant justice. As regards the rest, I think I quite understand you, although I do not, as yet, quite see into the closeness of the connection between those 'nature-tones' and music."

"Lewis answered--"Can the music which dwells within us be any other than that which lies buried in nature as a profound mystery, comprehensible only by the inner, higher sense, uttered by instruments, as the organs of it, merely in obedience to a mighty spell, of which we are the masters? But, in the purely psychical action and operation of the spirit--

that is to say, in dreams--this spell is broken; and then, in the tones of familiar instruments, we are enabled to recognise those nature-tones as wondrously engendered in the air, they come floating down to us, and swell and die away."

""'I think of the Æolian harp," said Ferdinand. "What is your opinion about that ingenious invention?"

""'Every attempt," said Lewis, "to tempt Nature to give forth her tones is glorious, and highly worthy of attention. Only, it seems to me that, as yet, we have only offered her trifling toys, which she has often shattered to pieces in her indignation. Much grander idea than all those playthings (like Æolian harps) was the 'storm harp' which I have read of. It was made of thick chords of wire, which were stretched out at considerable distances apart, in the open country, and gave forth great, powerful chords when the wind smote upon them.

""'Altogether, there is still a wide field open to thoughtful inventors in this direction, and I quite believe that the impulse recently given to natural science in general will be perceptible in this branch of it, and bring into practical existence much which is, as yet, nothing but speculation."

"Just at this moment there came suddenly floating through the air an extraordinary sound, which, as it swelled and became more distinguishable, seemed to resemble the tone of a harmonica. Lewis and Ferdinand stood rooted to the spot in amazement, not unmixed with awe; the tones took the form of a profoundly sorrowful melody sung by a female voice. Ferdinand grasped Lewis by the hand, whilst

41

the latter whisperingly repeated the words,

""'Mio ben, ricordati, s' avvien ch' io mora."

"'At the time when this occurred they were outside of the town, and before the entrance to a garden which was surrounded by lofty trees and tall hedges. There was a pretty little girl--whom they had not observed before--sitting playing in the grass near them, and she sprang up crying, "Oh, how beautifully my sister is singing again! I must take her some flowers, for she always sings sweeter and longer when she sees a beautiful carnation." And with that she gathered a bunch of flowers, and went skipping into the garden with it, leaving the gate ajar, so that our friends could see through it. What was their astonishment to see Professor X---- standing in the middle of the garden, beneath a lofty ash-tree! Instead of the repellant grin of irony with which he had received them at his house, his face wore an expression of deep melancholy earnestness, and his gaze was fixed upon the heavens, as if he were contemplating that world beyond the skies, whereof those marvellous tones, floating in the air like the breath of a zephyr, were telling. He walked up and down the central alley, with slow and measured steps; and, as he passed along, everything around him seemed to waken into life and movement. In every direction crystal tones came scintillating out of the dark bushes and trees, and, streaming through the air like flame, united in a wondrous concert, penetrating the inmost heart, and waking in the soul the most rapturous emotions of a higher world. Twilight was falling fast; the Professor disappeared among the hedges, and the tones died away in pianissimo. At length our friends went back to the town in profound silence; but, as Lewis was about to quit Ferdinand, the latter clasped him firmly, saying--

""'Be true to me! Do not abandon me! I feel, too clearly, some hostile foreign influence at work upon my whole existence, smiting upon all its hidden strings, and making them resound at its pleasure. I am helpless to resist it, though it should drive me to my destruction! Can that diabolical, sneering irony, with which the Professor received us at his house, have been anything other than the expression of this hostile principle? Was it with any other intention than that of getting his hands washed of me for ever, that he fobbed us off with those automatons of his?"

""'You are very probably right," said Lewis; "for I have a strong suspicion myself that, in some manner which is as yet an utter riddle to me, the Professor does exercise some sort of power or influence over your fate, or, I should rather say, over that mysterious psychical relationship, or affinity, which exists between you and this lady. It may be that, being mixed up in some way with this affinity, in his character of an element hostile to it, he strengthens it by the very fact that he opposes it: and it may also be that that which renders you so extremely unacceptable to him is the circumstance that your presence awakens, and sets into lively movement all the strings and chords of this mutually sympathetic condition, and this contrary to his desire, and, very probably, in opposition to some conventional family arrangement."

"'Our friends determined to leave no stone unturned in their efforts to make a closer approach to the Professor, with the hope that they might succeed, sooner or later, in clearing up this mystery which so affected Ferdinand's destiny and fate, and they were to have paid him a visit on the following morning as a preliminary step. However, a letter, which Ferdinand unexpectedly received from his father, summoned him to B----; it was impossible for him to permit himself the smallest delay, and in a few hours he was off, as fast as post-horses could convey him, assuring Lewis, as he started, that nothing should prevent his return in a fortnight, at the very furthest.

"'It struck Lewis as a singular circumstance that, soon after Ferdinand's departure, the same old gentleman who had at first spoken of the Professor's connection with "the Talking Turk," took an opportunity of enlarging to him on the fact that X----'s mechanical inventions were simply the result of an extreme enthusiasm for mechanical pursuits, and of deep and searching investigations in natural science; he also more particularly lauded the Professor's wonderful discoveries in music, which, he said, he had not as yet communicated to any one, adding that his mysterious laboratory was a pretty garden outside the town, and that passers by had often heard wondrous tones and melodies there, just as if the whole place were peopled by fays and spirits.

"'The fortnight elapsed, but Ferdinand did not come back. At length, when two months had gone by, a letter came from him to the following effect--

""Read and marvel; though you will learn only that which, perhaps, you strongly suspected would be the case, when you got to know more of the Professor--as I hope you did. As the horses were being changed in the village of P----, I was standing, gazing into the distance, not thinking specially of anything in particular. A carriage drove by, and stopped at the church, which was open. A young lady, simply dressed, stepped out of the carriage, followed by a young gentleman in a Russian Jaeger uniform, wearing several decorations; two gentlemen got down from a second carriage. The innkeeper said, 'Oh, this is the stranger couple our clergyman is marrying to-day.' Mechanically I went into the church, just as the clergyman was concluding the service with the blessing. I looked at the couple--the bride was my sweet singer. She looked at me, turned pale, and fainted. The gentleman who was behind her caught her in his arms. It was Professor X----. What happened further I do not know, nor have I any recollection as to how I got here; probably Professor X---- can tell you all about it. But a peace and a happiness, such as I have never known before, have now taken possession of my soul. The mysterious prophecy of the Turk was a cursed falsehood, a mere result of blind groping with unskilful antennæ. Have I lost her? Is she not mine for ever in the glowing inner life?

""It will be long ere you hear of me, for I am going on to K----, and perhaps to the extreme north, as far as P----."

"'Lewis gathered the distracted condition of his friend's mind, only too plainly, from his language, and the whole

45

affair became the greater a riddle to him when he ascertained that it was matter of certainty that Professor X---- had not quitted the town.

""How," thought he, "if all this be but a result of the conflict of mysterious psychical relations (existing, perhaps, between several people) making their way out into everyday life, and involving in their circle even outward events, independent of them, so that the deluded inner sense looks upon them as phenomena proceeding unconditionally from itself, and believes in them accordingly? It may be that the hopeful anticipation which I feel within me will be realised--for my friend's consolation. For the Turk's mysterious prophecy is fulfilled, and perhaps, through that very fulfilment, the mortal blow which menaced my friend is averted.""

"Well," said Ottmar, as Theodore came to a sudden stop, "is that all? Where is the explanation? What became of Ferdinand, the beautiful singer, Professor X----, and the Russian officer?"

"You know," said Theodore, "that I told you at the beginning that I was only going to read you a fragment, and I consider that the story of the Talking Turk is only of a fragmentary character, essentially. I mean, that the imagination of the reader, or listener, should merely receive one or two more or less powerful impulses, and then go on swinging, pendulum-like, of its own accord, as it chooses. But if you, Ottmar, are really anxious to have your mind set at rest over Ferdinand's future condition, remember the dialogue on opera which I read to you some time since. This is the same Ferdinand who appears therein, sound of mind and body; in the 'Talking Turk' he is at an earlier stage of his career. So that probably his somnambulistic love-affair ended satisfactorily enough."

"To which," said Ottmar, "has to be added that our Theodore used, at one time, to take a wonderful delight in exciting people's imaginations by means of the most extraordinary--nay, wild and insane--stories, and then suddenly break them off. Not only this, but everything he did, at that time, assumed a fragmentary form. He read second volumes only, not troubling himself about the firsts or thirds; saw only the second and third acts of plays; and so on."

"And," said Theodore, "that inclination I still have; to this hour nothing is so distasteful to me as when, in a story or a novel, the stage on which the imaginary world has been in action comes to be swept so clean by the historic besom that there is not the smallest grain or particle of dust left on it; when one goes home so completely sated and satisfied that one has not the faintest desire left to have another peep behind the curtain. On the other hand, many a fragment of a clever story sinks deep into my soul, and the continuance of the play of my imagination, as it goes along on its own swing, gives me an enduring pleasure. Who has not felt this over Goethe's 'Nut-brown Maid'! And, above all, his fragment of that most delightful tale of the little lady whom the traveller always carried about with him in a little box always exercises an indescribable charm upon me."

"Enough," interrupted Lothair. "We are not to hear any more about the Talking Turk, and the story was really all told, after all. So let Ottmar begin without more ado."

Ottmar took out his manuscript, and read:

www.ingramcontent.com/pod-product-compliance
Lightning Source LLC
Chambersburg PA
CBHW050311260626
47156CB00005B/1760

* 9 781447 465645 *